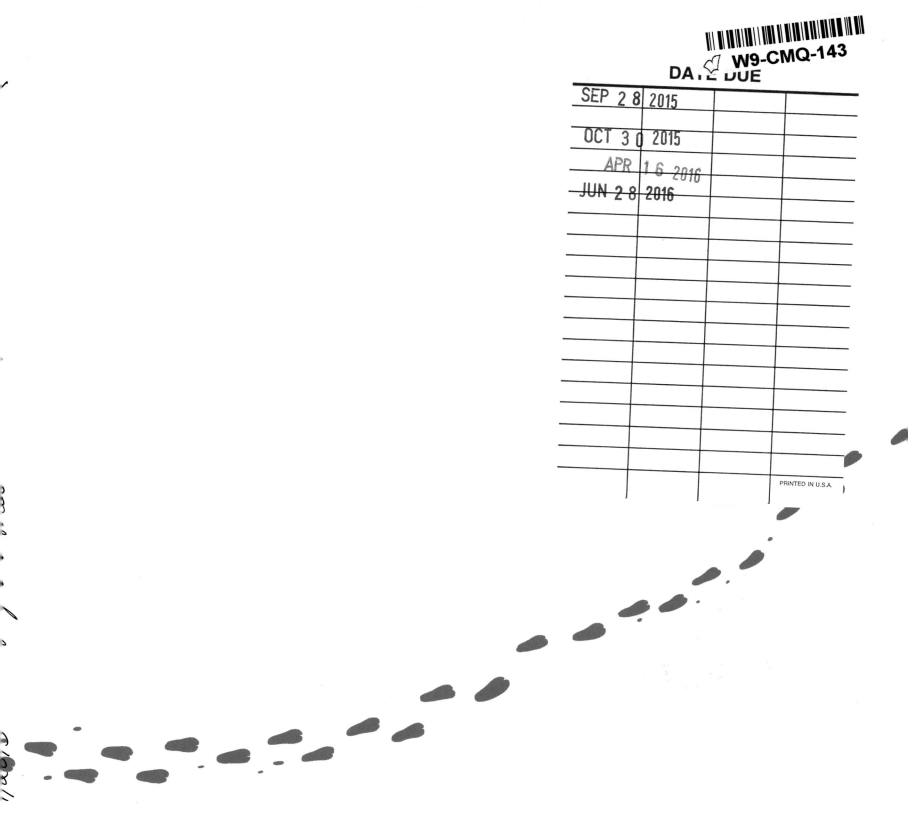

THERE'S A MOUSE HIDING IN THIS BOOK!

by Benjamin Bird

PICTURE WINDOW BOOKS
capstonepub.com

THERE'S A MOUSE HIDING IN THIS BOOK!
is published by Picture Window Books,
A Capstone Imprint
1710 Roe Crest Drive
North Mankato, Minnesota 56003
www.capstonepub.com

CAPS32265

Cataloging-in-Publication Data is available
on the Library of Congress website.
ISBN: 978-1-62370-125-3 (paper over board)
ISBN: 978-1-4795-5228-3 (library hardcover)
ISBN: 978-1-4795-6160-5 (eBook)

DESIGNED BY:
Russell Griesmer

ILLUSTRATED BY:
Comicup Studio
Carmen Pérez — Pencils
Francesc Figueres Farrès — Inks
Gloria Caballe — Color

Printed in the United States of America in North Mankato, Minnesota.
052014   008087CGF14

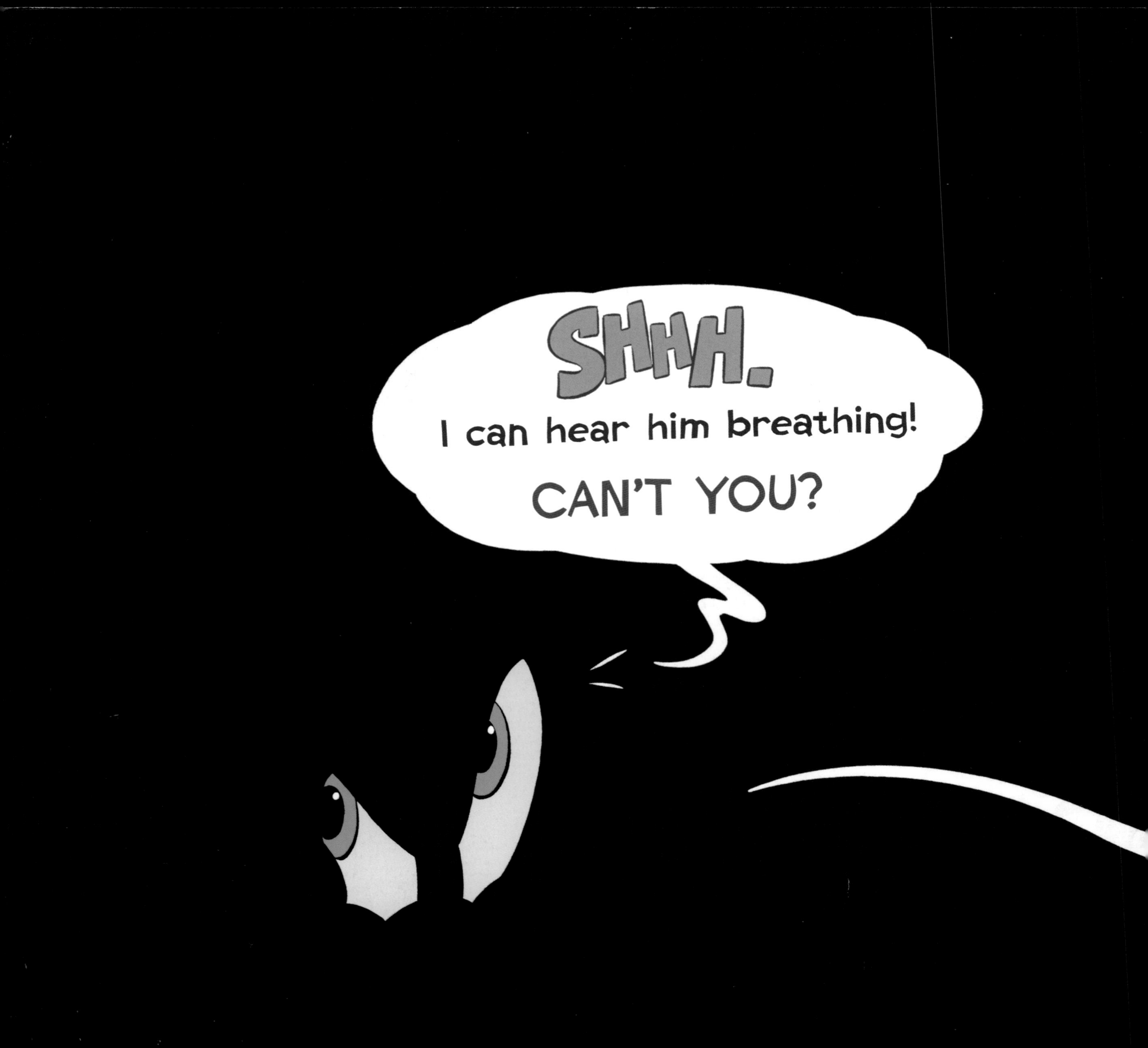
SHHH.
I can hear him breathing!
CAN'T YOU?

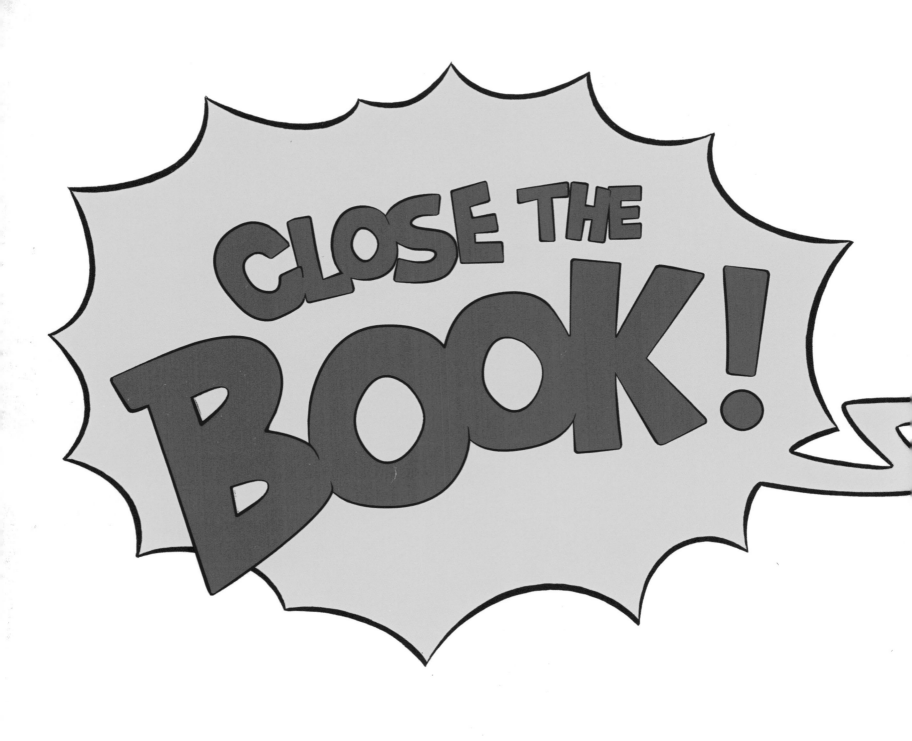